Thomas Flintham's Marvellous Mazes

SCHOLASTIC

For my Mum and Dad

www.thomasflintham.com

Scholastic Children's Books,
Euston House,
24 Eversholt Street,
London NW1 1DB, UK

A division of Scholastic Ltd
London ~ New York ~ Toronto ~ Sydney ~ Auckland
Mexico City ~ New Delhi ~ Hong Kong

Published in the UK by Scholastic Ltd, 2011

Text and illustrations © Thomas Flintham, 2011

All rights reserved

ISBN 978 1407 12088 1

Printed and bound by Tien Wah Press Pte. Ltd, Singapore

Welcome to Thomas Flintham's Marvellous Mazes! All kinds of super-amazing maze adventures await you inside the pages of this book. I hope you have lots of fun. Don't get lost!

Hello! We are the maze technicians. We're experts on everything there is to know about mazes.

→

We are going to fill you in on everything you need to know to solve the mazes in this book. Don't worry, it's all simple really.

↓

Each maze has a 'B' symbol, like this. This is the point in the maze you need to try to get to. When you have found your way to the 'B' symbol, you've solved the maze!

Every maze has an 'A' symbol and a 'B' symbol, and the aim of every maze is to get from the 'A' to the 'B'.

↙

The 'A' symbol marks where each maze starts. No matter what the maze looks like, you always start wherever the 'A' symbol is.

There are many different kinds of mazes in this book, and they don't all look the same. Don't worry though, there is an easy way to see how each maze works.

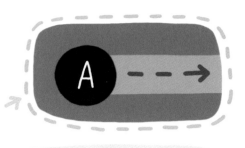

At the start of every maze, there is an arrow coming from the 'A' symbol. This arrow shows you where to start your route and is the key to understanding how each maze works. By looking at the arrow, and where it goes, you can work out which parts of the picture make up the maze.

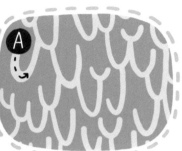

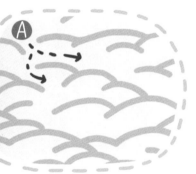

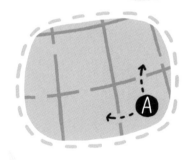

Here are some examples of the different kinds of mazes. See how the arrow shows you the way each maze works.

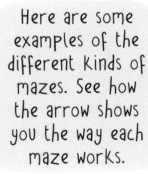

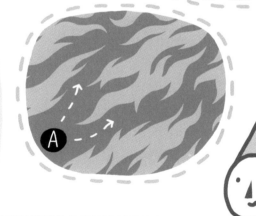

That should be all you need to know to solve the mazes. Some mazes are harder than others, so if you get stuck on a tricky one, why not leave it, try another one and come back to it later. Good luck, and have fun!

Welcome to Mazeland!

While you are here you will see wonderful sights and have some amazing adventures. Here is just a taste of what you have to look forward to:

No matter where you go in Mazeland there is always someone interesting to meet. The maze people all have one thing in common – they love solving mazes!

A

Keep an eye out for Astro Pete, Mazeland's number-one astronaut. You wouldn't believe the amazing things he's seen while exploring outer space!

Mazeland is full of heroes, just like the Little Knight, ready to take on its many adventures. He might be small, but he can easily deal with Mazeland's biggest challenges.

They're in the woods. They're even up the highest mountains. Mazeland is full of all sorts of animals, creatures and critters. How many will you see?

The one thing you'll find in Mazeland, no matter where you go, is mazes! They're everywhere! Hard ones and easy ones. Long ones and short ones. All kinds of mazes in all kinds of places! Please enjoy your visit to Mazeland, we hope that you enjoy seeing all the sights and solving all the mazes!

Turn the page to start your maze adventure!

The wolf howls in frustration at the moon and its tricky maze. No matter how hard he tries, he just can't solve it.

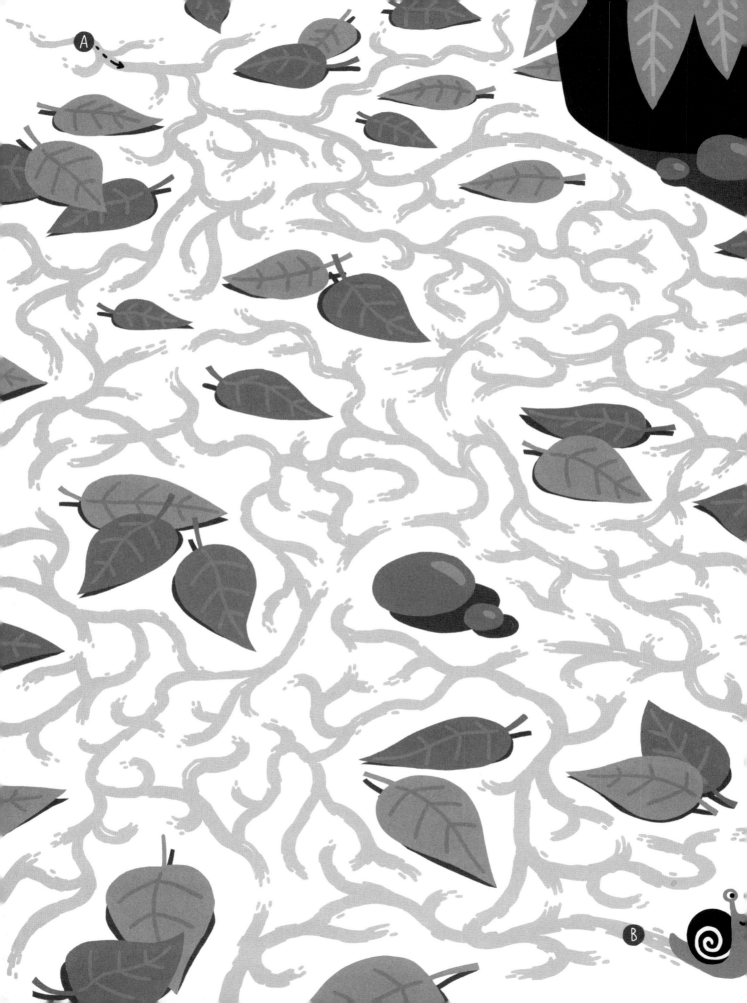

THE LITTLE KNIGHT
AND THE CURSED CROWN

One day the prince came to the Little Knight to ask for help with a royal emergency. The King had been turned into a monster!

A wizard had given the King the gift of a shiny new crown, but it was a trick! As soon as the King put on the crown he was transformed into a scary, hairy beast!

The prince fled the castle in fear. He knew the only person who could save the King and get the castle back from the wizard was the super-brave Little Knight.

The prince gave the Little Knight a map to the King's island, and without delay the land's smallest adventurer set out to save the day!

With a swish of his sword, the Little Knight chopped the wizard's magic wand in half, freeing himself and taking away the wizard's magical powers.

The now powerless wizard was captured and locked away inside the king's prison.

The cursed crown was locked away where it could do no more harm.

"Thank you so much, Little Knight," said the King. "If it wasn't for you I'd still be a monster and he would have taken over my whole kingdom. I can't thank you enough, little guy."

The Little Knight wasn't really listening though. He was busy thinking about how nice his shield would look with a maze painted on it. Don't be rude, Little Knight!

The End

Bethany's favourite pictures at the art gallery are the classical portrait paintings. She thinks this one is beautiful.

Ramona loves all the modern art at the gallery. She likes trying to figure out what each painting is about. This painting is called 'Scattered Well'. What could it mean?...

Hello! Are you enjoying the party?

Do you like my new hat? It's tops isn't it?

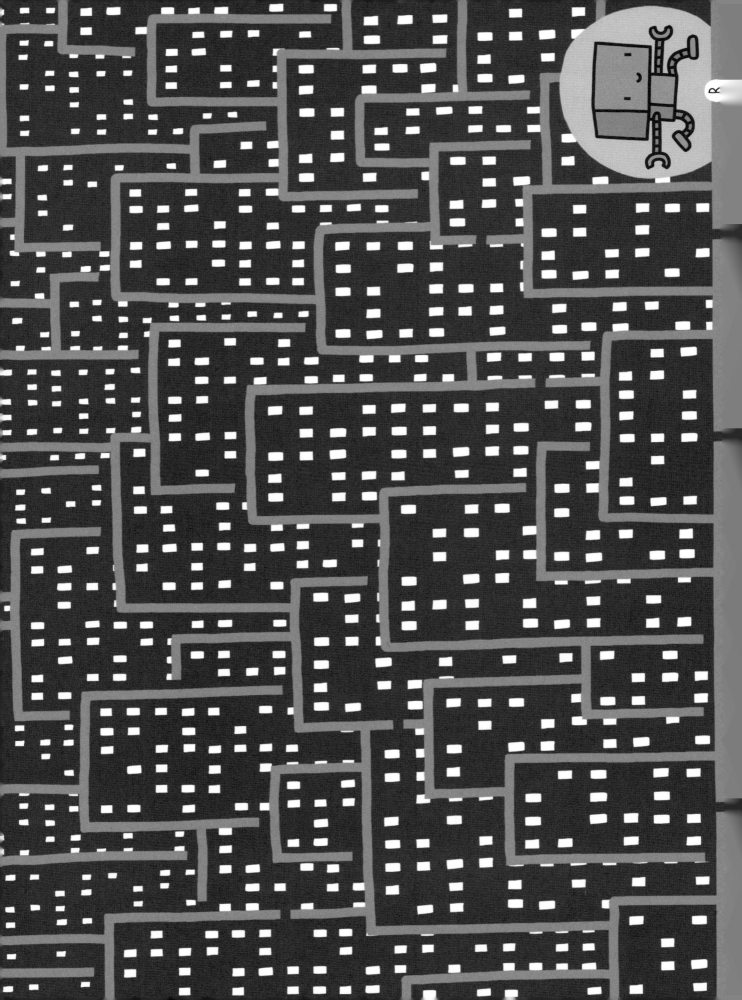

What do dogs dream about when they sleep?

THE ADVENTURES OF Astro Pete

THE PERFECT PLANET PROBLEM

Meet Astro Pete, legendary astronaut and space explorer. After many years of space adventures he has decided it's time to find a planet to make his home. Surely the perfect planet can't be too hard to find...

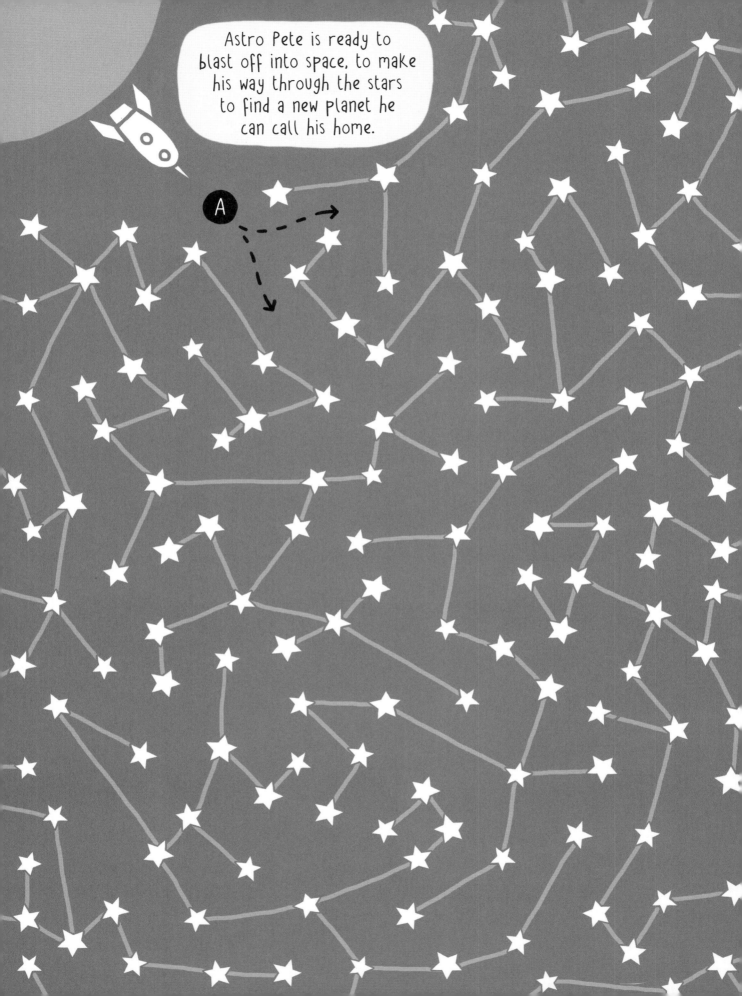

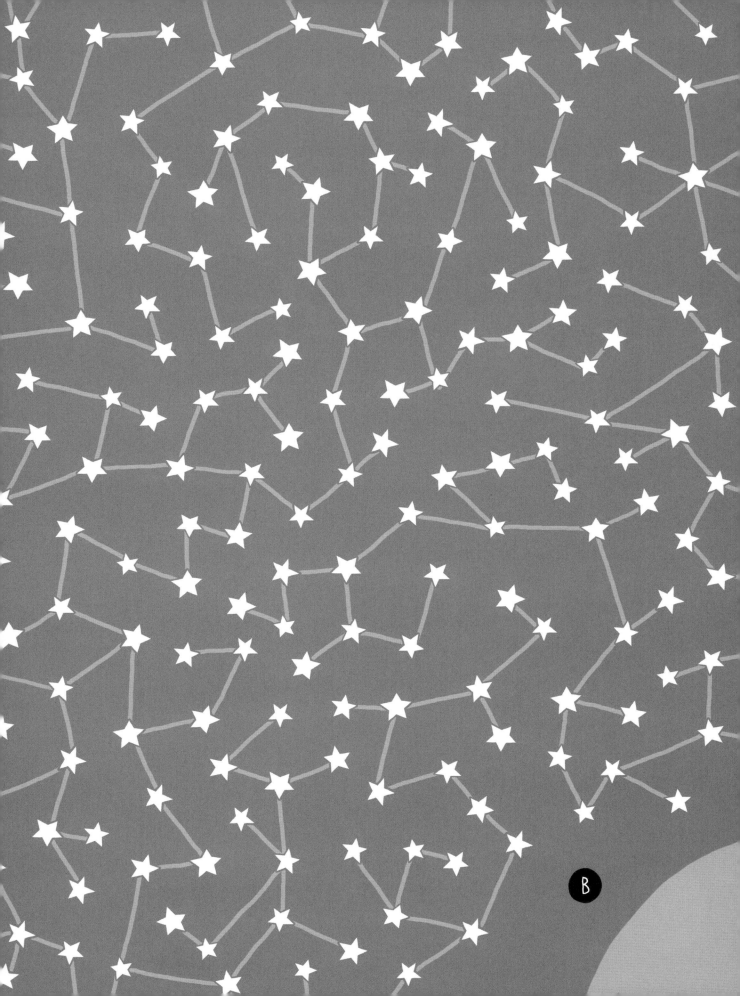

B

A

The Zondra
(very hungry)

Astro Pete
(Super-brave astronaut.
He's not afraid of
anything. Except giant
monsters, that is.)

The Planet Wist is hot. Very, very, very hot in fact. Far too hot for poor Astro Pete. After ten minutes on the planet he feels like he's about to melt! He'd better stick to the shadows and get back to his rocket before he becomes a barbecued astronaut!

Astro Pete thought he'd found the Perfect Planet, and it would have been perfect if it wasn't for all the noisy guys. Everyone who lived there was constantly shouting, yelling, crashing, banging, and stomping all over the place. Poor Astro Pete couldn't get any peace and quiet. Can he even find an escape route back to his rocket without someone shouting at him?

Astro Pete's been sucked into a wormhole! If he can make it through he'll find himself in a completely different part of space, with new planets to try. If he can make it out that is...

he Planet Bixxo
just too small.
on't give up
stro Pete, surely
e next planet
ll be better.

Astro Pete
(A normal-sized
guy, not a giant
despite how it
might look.)

Planet
Bixxo's moon
(Also small)

Astro Pete's
Space Boots
(size 8)

A

Flowers
(Not trees)

B

Space snail
(Same size as a
normal snail.)

As Astro Pete approaches another planet, he is hopeful that this time he has found the perfect place to live. Is this the new home he has been looking for all this time? There is only one way for him to find out, and that is to land and have a good look around. Good luck, Astro Pete!

The Planet Sneep is a very crowded place. The whole planet is covered in super-tall skyscrapers and massive, endless crowds of people. Within a week of living there, Astro Pete was fed up of being constantly overcrowded and surrounded all the time, with no open space on the whole planet where he could take a break from it all. He decided it was time to make his way through the crowds, back to his rocket to continue his search. Poor Astro Pete.

After a long and unsuccessful search, Astro Pete found himself back where he had started on the Planet Bib.

After his adventures, Planet Bib seemed very different. It was still very dull, but that didn't seem so bad anymore.

It wasn't too scary.

It wasn't too hot.

It wasn't too loud.

And it wasn't too crowded.

Astro Pete decided that Planet Bib wasn't a bad place to live after all. Yes it was a bit dull, but that was what made it the perfect place for him to rest in between all his many exciting space adventures. Astro Pete loves to return home for a bit of a break, with nothing else to do but relax and solve some of the Moon's mazes. He's found the perfect home at last!

Fox in the snow, where will you go to find something nice to eat? Why not have a look in that bin?

The mouse needs to get back to his mouse hole without being seen by the hungry owl. He should probably stay in the shadows to be safe.

A field full of hungry crows is not a nice place for a little worm to live. If the worm can make it to the scarecrow he should be safe from harm. Watch out for those crows!

Far, far away
in the deepest forest
at the top of the tallest
trees, sits King Wishing-bird.
If you were to find him and
tap his magic crown, he would
grant you any wish you could
ask. Provided you ask very
nicely and feed him lots
of chocolate.

Daniel has an imaginary friend called Mr Huss. Mr Huss is very good at hide and seek and storytelling and likes to help Daniel to solve mazes. When they work together there is no maze they can't beat!

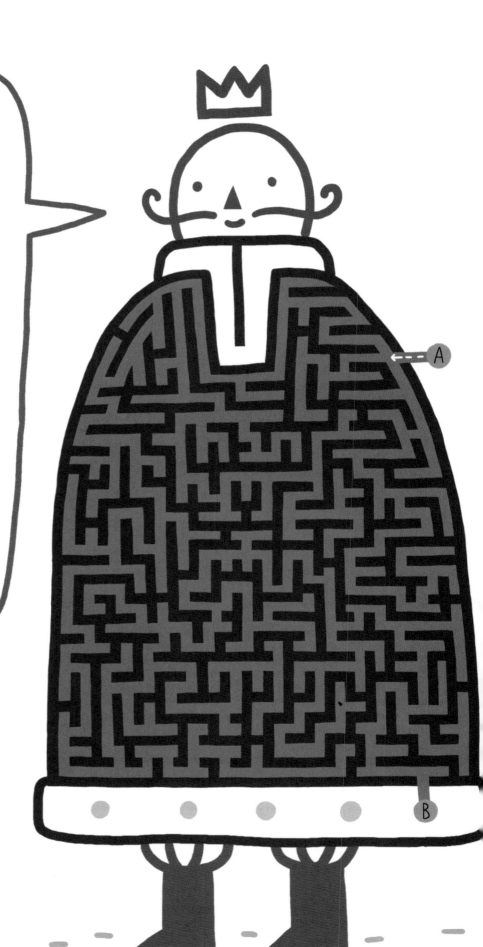